IT'S NOT ABOUT THE APPLE!

Veronika Martenova Charles

Illustrated by David Parkins

TUNDRA BOOKS

Published in Canada by Tundra Books,
75 Sherbourne Street, Toronto, Ontario M5A 2P9

Published in the United States by Tundra Books of Northern New York,
P.O. Box 1030, Plattsburgh, New York 12901

Library of Congress Control Number: 2009938094

Library and Archives Canada Cataloguing in Publication

Charles, Veronika Martenova
    It's not about the apple! / Veronika Martenova
Charles ; illustrated by David Parkins.

(Easy-to-read wonder tales)
ISBN 978-0-88776-955-9

    1. Fairy tales. 2. Children's stories, Canadian (English).
I. Parkins, David II. Title. III. Series: Charles, Veronika
Martenova. Easy-to-read wonder tales.

PS8555.H42242I87 2010   jC813'.54   C2009-905857-X

We acknowledge the financial support of the Government of Canada through
the Book Publishing Industry Development Program (BPIDP) and that of the
Government of Ontario through the Ontario Media Development Corporation's
Ontario Book Initiative. We further acknowledge the support of the Canada Council
for the Arts and the Ontario Arts Council for our publishing program.

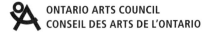

ONTARIO ARTS COUNCIL
CONSEIL DES ARTS DE L'ONTARIO

CONTENTS

In the Schoolyard Part 1   4

Three Sisters   6
  (*Snow White* from Greece)

The Stone of Patience   24
  (*Snow White* from Armenia)

Bianca and the Six Robbers   42
  (*Snow White* from Italy)

In the Schoolyard Part 2   60

About the Stories   64

IN THE SCHOOLYARD
PART 1

"Look!" said Lily

to Ben and Jake.

"Somebody forgot a lunch box.

There is an apple in it.

I think I'll have a bite."

"Don't eat that!" said Jake.

"It could be poisoned,

and you could die

like Snow White in the story."

"That's not how the story goes,"

said Ben.

"It was a poisoned ring,

not a poisoned apple.

And Snow White wasn't dead.

She was only sleeping.

I'll tell you the story."

THREE SISTERS

(*Snow White* from Greece)

Once, there were three sisters

who were orphans.

One morning they went out

to watch the sunrise.

"Sun, who is the best of us all?"

the eldest sister asked.

And the sun replied,

"One is as good as the other,

but the youngest is best of all."

The two elder sisters' hearts filled

with envy when they heard that.

They made a plan to get rid of

their younger sister, Kay.

"Our mother has been dead

for years," they told Kay.

"It's time she had a proper grave.

Tomorrow, we must go up

to the mountains and rebury her."

Kay believed them and baked

some bread to eat along the way.

The next morning, the sisters set off.

They walked through the mountains

and stopped under a tree.

The eldest sister said,

"This is where our mother lies.

Give me the shovel."

"Oh dear," the middle sister said,

"we forgot to bring one.

Kay, you stay here while

we go and get the shovel."

And the older two left Kay alone.

Kay waited until the sun set.

Then she began to cry.

"Don't cry," a tree told her.

"Drop the bread you're holding

and follow where it goes.

You will find a place to stay."

Kay let the bread roll down

the mountain.

It led her to a canyon.

There was a house

carved into the mountainside.

Kay went in, but no one was home.

She found huge pots in the kitchen

and food in the cellar.

So she cooked a delicious meal,

ate a little, and then fell asleep

inside a cupboard.

At midnight, three giants came in.

"Who has done this for us?"

they asked.

"Don't be afraid to come out.

If you are a man, be our brother.

If you are a woman, be our sister."

14

Kay heard this and climbed

out of the cupboard.

"So it was you who made this

delicious meal," the giants said.

"You're welcome to stay with us

and be in charge of our house."

The next time Kay's sisters asked

who was the best,

the sun gave the same reply.

"Kay must still be alive.

Let's get rid of her for good."

The sisters made a poisoned ring

and returned to the mountains.

They searched everywhere until

they found the giants' house.

Rat-tat! They knocked on the door.

"Are you there, Kay?

It's us, your sisters."

Kay opened the door.

"We brought you a present,"

said her sisters.

They gave Kay the ring.

When she put it on, she fainted.

That night, the giants found Kay

crumpled on the ground.

They couldn't revive her,

so they put her in a golden casket

and floated it down the river.

As it happened,

a prince rode by on the riverbank

just as the box drifted past.

Curious, he pulled it out

and took it to his palace.

There, he opened the golden box

and found the lifeless girl inside.

The prince saw the poisoned ring.

Maybe her name is on it,

he thought. When he pulled

the ring off her finger to see,

Kay sighed and started to breathe.

She told the prince what happened,

and he was touched by her tale.

"Please stay and marry me,"

the prince said.

When the sisters found out

Kay was alive and a prince's bride,

their hearts burned up with envy,

and no one heard from them again.

"I wonder," said Jake, "if those giants were miners like the dwarfs in the *Snow White* movie."

"No, you need to be little to crawl in tunnels," said Ben.

"I think giants build mountains, and dwarfs dig through them."

"I also know a story about a girl who goes to a house in the woods like Snow White," said Lily. "But there are no giants or dwarfs."

"So, who lives there?" asked Ben.

"Listen to the story," said Lily.

★

THE STONE OF PATIENCE

(*Snow White* from Armenia)

There was once a rich man

who had a daughter, Anel,

and a beautiful, new wife.

Each month when there was

a new moon,

the wife asked,

"Moon, am I the most beautiful?"

And the moon replied,

"You are the most beautiful."

But when Anel was ten years old,

the new moon told the wife,

"It is Anel, your stepdaughter,

who is the most beautiful of all."

Instead of being pleased,

the wife was very jealous.

"Who is more important to you?"

she asked her husband.

"Is it me or your daughter?

You can't have us both.

You must get rid of Anel."

The father was very sad.

"Anel, come with me,"

he told his little girl.

After they walked for miles,

the father gave Anel a warm coat.

"Now run away to someplace safe!"

he told her. Then he left.

Anel wandered through the woods

until she came to a large house.

Perhaps this is a safe place,

she thought.

She put her hand on the door,

and it opened.

Anel walked in,

and the door disappeared.

There was a room full of gold

and another one full of silver.

In another room Anel found

a boy sleeping. She called to him,

but he did not answer.

Then she heard a voice.

"For seven years

you must look after this boy

and prepare his food."

For the next four years,

Anel took care of the boy.

One day, Anel looked outside

and saw a band of gypsies.

"I'm lonely up here," she called.

"Is there a girl about my age

who would like to stay with me?"

The gypsies threw a rope up to

the window and a girl climbed in.

The girls soon became friends

and took turns caring for the boy.

First, Anel would look after him,

and next, the gypsy girl would.

So it went for three more years.

"Then one day, while the gypsy girl

was fanning the boy, he awoke.

"So, it is you who cared for me!"

he said. "As a reward,

I want you to be my princess."

"If you wish, I will," replied

the gypsy girl.

Anel heard them and was bitter.

As they prepared for the wedding,

the prince said to Anel,

"You also must have helped

take care of me a little.

What present would you like?"

"Bring me a *saber dashee* stone,"

Anel answered.

The prince went to town,

bought the wedding gown,

and then went to a stonecutter.

"Who is this stone for?"

the stonecutter asked.

"It's for my servant,"

said the prince.

"This is a stone of patience,"

the stonecutter said.

"If someone has great troubles

and tells them to the *saber dashee,*

it eases their pain.

But if the stone can't bear

the sorrow, it swells and bursts.

Your servant must have

an important story to tell."

That night the prince stayed

outside of Anel's door to listen

as she talked to the stone.

She spoke of her cruel stepmother

who drove her away

and about the seven long years

she spent taking care of the boy.

She asked, "Tell me, *saber dashee*,

am I more patient than you?"

The stone began to swell.

Then she told the stone

how her gypsy friend didn't say

one word about all the time

Anel had looked after the prince.

The prince entered the room.

Just then, the *saber dashee* burst.

"Anel," said the prince,

"I didn't know the whole story.

It's you who should be my wife."

So Anel and the prince got married.

"I wonder, what happened to that

gypsy girl," said Ben.

"Maybe she moved out and

went traveling," said Lily.

"And she sent pictures

of far-off places to Anel,

because they were still friends."

"I know another story about a girl

who has to run away and hide,"

said Jake, "and she ends up

living with robbers!"

"How?" asked Lily and Ben.

"Listen, I'll tell you," said Jake.

★

BIANCA AND SIX ROBBERS

(*Snow White* from Italy)

Once, a mother and daughter

had an inn by the road.

While travelers sat at the tables,

the mother would ask them,

"Have you ever seen a face

more beautiful than mine?"

"No, I have not,"

each traveler would answer.

But one day when the mother

asked her question, Bianca,

her daughter, walked by.

"Yes, I have," the man replied.

"This girl's face is lovelier."

That evening the mother

called the kitchen boy.

"Go to the seashore,

build a hut with one tiny window,

and shut my daughter in it,"

she told him.

The kitchen boy built the hut

and took Bianca to it.

But he didn't have the heart

to close her up inside.

"Run!" he told her,

"and don't ever come back!"

Bianca ran into the woods.

It was a gloomy, rocky place.

After a time, she heard voices.

She hid behind a tree,

and soon she saw six robbers

standing beside a white boulder.

One of them said, "Open, cave!"

and the boulder swung open.

From inside there was a glow.

After the robbers entered,

the last one said, "Close, cave!"

and the boulder closed.

Bianca hid until the robbers left.

Then she called, "Open, cave!"

and she stepped inside.

She saw six chickens on a spit

and a table laid for six.

Bianca tidied up the place

and roasted the chickens.

She was hungry and took

one bite out of every chicken.

Then she hid under a bed.

"Someone was here," the robbers

said when they returned.

"One of us should stand guard."

The following day,

one robber stayed behind

and pretended to be sleeping.

When Bianca came out of hiding,

he caught her.

"Don't be afraid," he said.

"You may stay if you like.

We will treat you as our sister."

So Bianca stayed with the robbers,

and she cooked for them.

A while later, one of the robbers

stopped at the inn by the road.

"Have you ever seen a face

more beautiful than mine?"

Bianca's mother asked.

"Yes. The face of the girl who

lives with us," said the robber.

Bianca must still be alive,

thought her mother.

"Anyone that beautiful," she said,

"deserves a special gift."

She gave him a golden hairpin.

It was filled with poison.

"I brought you a gift," the robber

told Bianca, when he returned.

She put the golden pin in her hair,

and soon she was dizzy and weak.

Then she stopped breathing.

The robbers thought
that Bianca was dead.
Still, she was so beautiful that
they didn't want to bury her,
so they chose a hollow tree
and put her inside.

Later, a prince was hunting

in the woods.

His dog stopped at the tree

and began to bark.

The prince looked inside and saw

the beautiful girl lying dead.

"If only you were alive, I would

ask you to marry me," he sighed.

The prince had the tree cut down

and taken to his palace

with the girl still inside.

There, he put her in a room,

so he could admire her beauty.

His sisters were curious and

snuck into the room.

"Look!" they said. "It is a doll!

Let's fix her hair."

As they combed Bianca's hair,

the golden pin fell out.

And Bianca woke up!

Everyone was surprised —

most of all, the prince.

He asked Bianca to marry him.

When her mother found out that

Bianca was to become a queen,

she went mad and lost her beauty.

And that was the end of her.

IN THE SCHOOLYARD
PART 2

"It served her right

for being so cruel!" said Ben,

after Jake finished his story.

"We should take the lunch box

to the office.

Someone must be looking for it."

Jake, Lily, and Ben went back

into the school

and handed the lunch box

to the school secretary.

"Thanks, kids," she said.

"I'll put it in the announcements tomorrow morning."

"Oh, by the way," Jake told her, "the apple could be poisoned, so no one should eat it."

The secretary looked confused.

Then she said, "I see. You mean

like in the story of *Snow White*!

But if I ate the poisoned apple

a prince might kiss me, right?

I wouldn't mind that," she laughed.

When they left, Ben said,

"That's not how the story goes."

"Well," said Jake, "in the movie,

the prince kisses Snow White

to break the spell.

I have it at home."

"Can we watch it?" asked Lily.

"Sure," said Jake. "Let's go!"

And so they went.

ABOUT THE STORIES

Snow White and the Seven Dwarfs was made popular by Walt Disney in 1937, as the first animated feature film. But similar stories already existed in many parts of the world. In some, there are giants or robbers instead of dwarfs.

Three Sisters is based on a story from Greece, called *Myrsina or Myrtle.*

The Stone of Patience comes from Armenia, and it is based on a story called *Nourie Hadig.*

Bianca and Six Robbers is inspired by the Italian tale, *Bella Venezia.*